Grandpa was Bullied

DARLENE JOHNSON CARGILL

To order additional copies of this book, contact:
Xlibris
844-714-8691
www.Xlibris.com
Orders@Xlibris.com

ISBN: Softcover   978-1-6698-1680-5
        Hardcover   978-1-6698-1681-2
        EBook   978-1-6698-1679-9

Print information available on the last page

Rev. date: 03/29/2022

Dedication:

This book is dedicated to the loving memory of Frequette Pursley who was a dear grandfather to all his grandchildren, especially his first grandson Ken Johnson Jr. And, to those grandfathers who are making a difference in the lives of their grandchildren everyday like Marshall Johnson, Nate Pursley, Fred Pursley, Gilbert Cargill and Glenn Waller, to name a few.

Also, in rememberance of heavenly grandfathers Rick Pursley and Ronald Appling.

"It's Saturday!" Tommy yelled as he threw off his bed covers.

Saturday was his favorite day of the week, for only one reason...he got to visit with his grandfather.

Tommy appeared to leap out of bed and run into the bathroom. He hurriedly brushed his teeth and splashed water on his face.

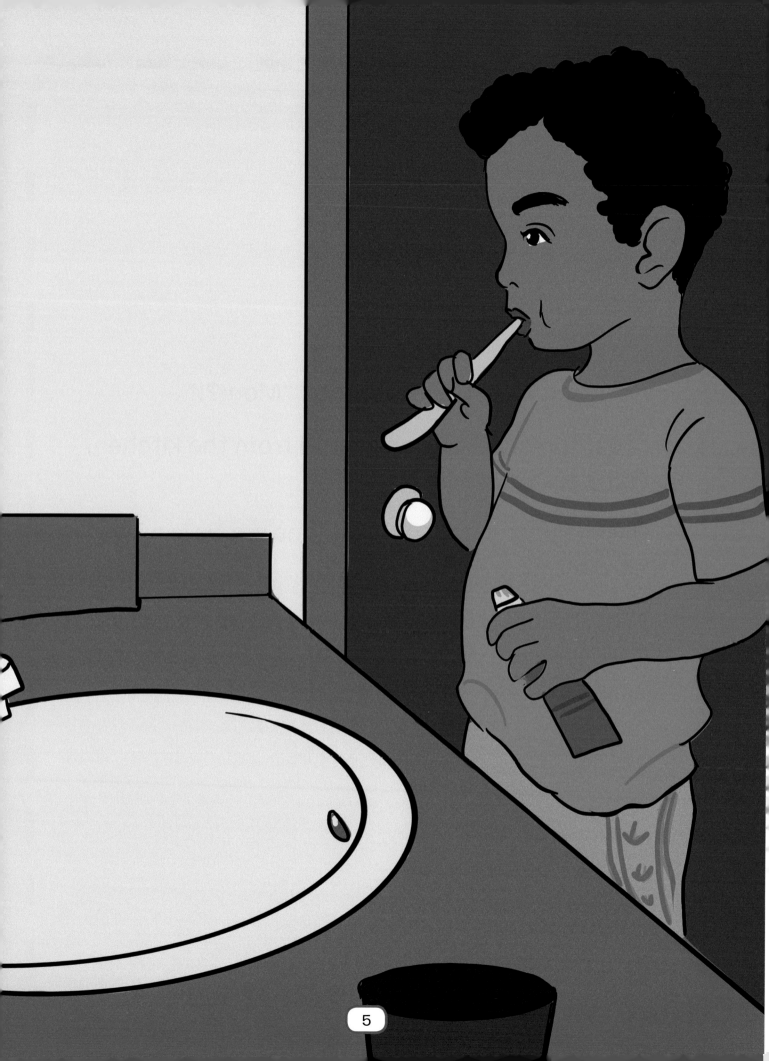

He yelled from the bathroom, "Mom?!"

"Yes, Tommy?" she answered from the kitchen. "Why are you yelling?"

"Is breakfast ready and what time are we leaving?" he wanted to know.

"Yes, breakfast is almost ready. C'mon and eat first and we'll discuss it at the table," came her answer.

Tommy hurriedly dressed and came to the breakfast table wearing jeans, a blue sweatshirt and untied tennis shoes.

Tommy's mom began to serve him his favorite breakfast.

"Mom," he said with fork raised in his hand and gulping a mouth full of food.

"Don't talk with food in your mouth," she answered.

Tommy swallowed and began again.

"Mom, I'm ready to go visit my grandfather now," he said.

"We'll go in an hour or so was her answer. "That will give you enough time to finish breakfast, clean your room and gather your dirty clothes for the laundry."

"Aww, mom, Tommy responded. "Papa, referring to his beloved grandfather, "always has chores for me to do when I get to his house."

"And you have chores to do here at home before you leave for his house," his mom said smiling.

"Take your time eating and we'll be out of here before you know it," she said.

Tommy continued to eat his breakfast in a hurry.

Tommy had a small frame which made him look younger than his 10 years. But he often wondered why his feet were not so small. He wore a size 9 1/2 shoe already which caused some of the boys at school to tease him because of his shoe size.

But his shoe size wasn't on his mind that morning.

Tommy was a curious kid and would spend hours by himself. He loved putting together jigsaw puzzles, reading books and playing computer games while at home.

While at school some of the bigger boys sometimes teased him because he was by himself, most of the time.

During recess he often sat on the designated "buddy bench" where the kids who didn't have anyone to play with sat.

Because of that, some of the bigger boys at school started to bully him. They called him a baby, even though he didn't think he acted like one. He was even called "Bigfoot."

To be called names really bothered him. He didn't like being called anything other than Tommy but he didn't know what to do about it.

Today, he planned to tell his grandfather about the name-calling he experienced at school. He believed his papa would know what to do.

More than anything, Tommy loved talking to his grandfather and listening to stories he shared.

And, he particularly loved hearing about his grandfather's experiences growing up. Some Saturdays they spent all afternoon just talking.

Later that morning just before noon, Tommy finally arrived at his grandfather's house when his papa was just finishing breakfast.

"Come here big boy and give your Papa a hug."

Tommy couldn't stop smiling and he gave him the biggest hug a boy his size could give.

His grandfather invited him to sit with him at the table while he finished his coffee. He poured Tommy a glass of orange juice.

Sitting at the table across from one another, Tommy began.

"Papa when you were a little boy were you ever called names by other kids?"

"Yes, said his grandfather. "I used to be called a lot of names."

"Were you afraid of the big boys? Tommy wanted to know.

"Some of them, he answered. "When I was your age, I was afraid of a lot of things."

"Like what?" Tommy wanted to know.

His grandfather began to tell Tommy his childhood fears.

"I was afraid of the dark, strange noises, spiders, you name it.

"Sometimes at night when the lights were turned off, I would hide under the covers and when I peeked out, it was daylight and the sun was shining through my window.

"Then when I was almost a teenager, I began to be unafraid of the dark.

"As a little boy, a few years younger than you are now, I was afraid of thunderstorms. I would sit on the couch hugging my blanket, sometimes I pulled it around my ears to block the rumbling sounds of the thunder.

"Then when the thunder stopped, I ran to the window and looked out. The only sounds I could hear were those of birds chirping and crickets singing. I loved the warmth from the sun on my face after a thunderstorm.

"Another thing I was afraid of was the sound of sirens from police and fire trucks. I would cover my ears if one was going by. Then one day I heard a firetruck stop on my street. I ran outside and watched as the firemen ran into a house a few doors away from mine. I watched the fireman pull someone out of the burning house. After that, I even wanted to be a fireman!

"I bet you wouldn't believe I used to be afraid of doctors. I remember my mom took me to get vaccinated when I started school. It hurt but only for a few minutes. My mom, your great grandmother, told me that vaccinations would prevent me from getting very sick. She was right, you know.

"Later when I was around your age, I learned not to be afraid of water because while away at summer camp, I learned to swim. The following year at camp I dived into the deep end of the pool. That was scary but I did it anyway.

"And while at school, I was afraid to ask others if I could join their team and play whatever game they were playing. I learned a lot about sports and that it is more fun to be on a team than sit and watch others playing.

"I was bullied when I was your age because I had trouble pronouncing certain words. The bully in my class made fun of me. One day he got in my face and I pushed him away. He punched me and I punched him back. We exchanged punches until the teacher broke us up. After that fight, no one was really hurt, he never bothered me again.

"Way back when, some of the kids made fun of how I dressed. My family didn't have much money to buy me a lot of clothes. But my clothes were always clean.

"I told my dad, your great grandfather, about the bullying and he told me bullies like to pretend that they are tough. He said the bullies are the ones who are really afraid and are not good at naming their fears. Instead, they pretend to be tough. He said bullies who hurt other people are hurting or have been hurt.

"I remember the times when I was really afraid, my mom would give me a hug and say I love you and there is nothing to be afraid of. I believed her because she was so smart. Your great grandmother and great grandfather were both right."

"I love you son," his grandfather said while looking straight into Tommy's eyes as he got up from the table.

His grandfather reached for him and gave him a big Papa hug and smiled.

Tommy looked up at his grandfather and said, "I love you too and I'm going to be like you when I'm a teenager."

His grandfather smiled.

"Tommy, son, just be the best you you can be at whatever age and don't focus so much on what others think and say about you. Names are just words and they can't hurt you. Believe in yourself. I believe you will do what's right. You know you can be anything you want to be and you're not what or who others say you are. If you just believe that, you would make your Papa very happy.

"Now, come and help me paint the garage," he said.

Tommy looked up at him and asked, "Papa, what size shoe did you wear when you were my age?"

"Oh! said his grandfather with a wink, "I recall it was a size 10. Now tie up your shoes."

Tommy smiled, reached down and
tied his shoes and off they went,
loaded with paint and brushes.

Printed in the United States
by Baker & Taylor Publisher Services